There's a Baby On The Way!

ISBN 978-0-99703-361-8

To my beloved husband, Collis III, thank you for completing me. My Mother, Mauretta, who instilled the importance of family and perserverance. My children, Monet, Eden, and Collis IV who inspire me every day and who are the inspiration for my books.

I found out today that I would soon have a baby sister.

I'm not sure if I should be happy or sad.

I don't want my mommy and
daddy to forget about me.

What if they don't want me anymore?

Daddy entered my room and said,
"Monet, please pick up all of your toys."

"Yes Sir," I replied.

"I will pick up all of my toys everyday,
never cry about anything else,
and promise to be a good little girl
forever daddy."

"You should always pick up your toys, it's okay to cry sometimes, and you are a good little girl. Where is this coming from Monet?" he said appearing confused.

"Nowhere, Daddy, nowhere," I replied.

Granny was in the kitchen cooking some red beans and rice, my favorite, and says, "I can't believe that I've run out of Creole Spice," it's her favorite seasoning.

"Granny, I don't need to have any seasoning in my food, matter of fact, I don't need to eat anymore." I said.

"My child, you must eat to live, and I can always go to the store and buy more seasoning. Where is this coming from Monet?"

"Nowhere,Granny, nowhere."

I ran out of the kitchen and into the living room, where my mommy was putting some of my clothes in a box, and became very concerned.

"Oh no, she's packing my clothes!
I will have to leave soon," I thought.

"Mommy," I called out, "I don't need any more clothes. I can wear the same clothes forever."

Mommy asked, "Where is this coming from Monet?"

"Nowhere, Mommy, nowhere."

Daddy decided to talk to me about what I'd said. "What made you say those things?"

"I don't want you to forget about me when the baby comes," I replied.

"Monet, I love you, and I would never forget about you. You will always be my Princess, and can never be replaced."

Granny called me to her room and asked
"What in the world would make
you think that you didn't need to eat?"

"I don't want you to send me away because
there is not enough food for me and the baby."

"Monet, I love you. The baby needs food, and
so do you. There is more than enough food
for the both of you. You will always be my Princess,
and can never be replaced."

Mommy was tucking me into bed and asked,
"What's the matter Monet, and why would you
think that you didn't need any more clothes?"

"I don't want you to send me away because the
baby needs clothes."

"Monet, I love you. The baby needs clothes, but so
do you. The clothes in the box are too small for you.
You will always be my Princess, and can never
be replaced."

Gee, even though there's a baby on the way,
I learned that there are enough toys, clothes, food,
and love for me and the baby; but most importantly,
I am their Princess, and could never be replaced.

The End.